For Janey

First U.S. Edition 1990

Published in Great Britain in 1990 by Frances Lincoln Limited

ISBN 0-316-51292-3
Library of Congress Catalog Card Number 90-53154
Library of Congress Cataloging-in-Publication information is available.

Joy Street Books are published by Little, Brown and Company (Inc.).

10 9 8 7 6 5 4 3 2 1

Printed in Great Britain

Ring-a-Round-a-Rosy

Nursery Rhymes, Action Rhymes and Lullabies

Illustrated by Priscilla Lamont

JOY STREET BOOKS

Little, Brown and Company
Boston   Toronto   London

·CONTENTS·

ACTION RHYMES

NURSERY RHYMES

LULLABIES

MUSIC FOR LULLABIES   **66**

Action Rhymes

Row, row, row your boat
Gently down the stream,
Merrily, merrily, merrily, merrily,
Life is but a dream.

This little piggy went to market,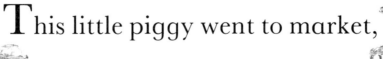

This little piggy stayed home,

This little piggy had roast beef,

This little piggy had none.

This little piggy cried, "Wee-wee-wee,"
All the way home.

Round and round the garden,
Like a teddy bear.
One step,
Two step,
And tickly under there!

Pat-a-cake, pat-a-cake, baker's man,
Bake me a cake as fast as you can.
Pat it and prick it and mark it with B,
And put it in the oven for Baby and me.

One, two, three, four, five,
Once I caught a fish alive.

Six, seven, eight, nine, ten,
Then I let it go again.

Why did you let it go?
Because it bit my finger so.

Which finger did it bite?
This little finger on my right.

Two little dicky birds
Sat upon a wall,
One named Peter,
The other named Paul.

Fly away, Peter!
Fly away, Paul!
Come back, Peter,
Come back, Paul.

Two little eyes to look around,
Two little ears to hear each sound,
One little nose to smell what's sweet,
One little mouth that likes to eat.

15

This is the way the lady rides,
Trit, trot, trit, trot.
This is the way the lady rides,
Trit, trit, trot.

This is the way the gentleman rides,
Trit-trot, trit-trot, trit-trot, trit-trot.
This is the way the gentleman rides,
Trit-trot, trit-trot, trit-trot.

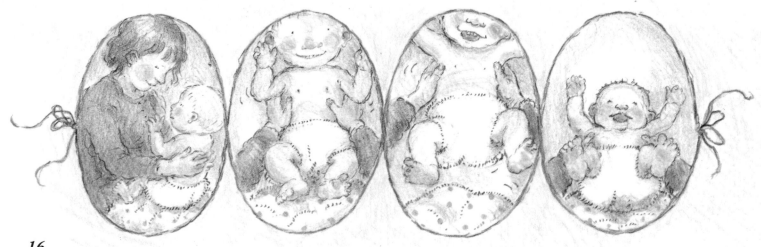

This is the way the farmer rides,
Gall-op, gall-op, gall-op, gall-op,
This is the way the farmer rides,
Gall-op, gall-op, gall-op.

This is the way the old man rides,
Hobble-dy, hobble-dy, hobble-dy,
And down into the ditch!

bloomin' horse!

Here's a ball for baby,
Big and soft and round,
Here is baby's hammer,
See how she can pound.

Here is baby's music,
Clapping, clapping, so.
Here are baby's soldiers,
Standing in a row.

Here is her umbrella
To keep our baby dry.
Here is baby's cradle
To rock-a-baby-bye.

18

Here we go round the mulberry bush,
The mulberry bush, the mulberry bush.
Here we go round the mulberry bush
So early in the morning.

This the way we brush our hair,
Brush our hair, brush our hair.
This is the way we brush our hair
So early in the morning.

This is the way we clean our teeth, etc.

This is the way we wash our hands, etc.

Ring-a-round-a-rosy,
A pocket full of posies,
Ashes! Ashes!
We all fall down.

Picking up the daisies,
Picking up the daisies,
Ashes! Ashes!
We all jump up.

21

This little cow eats grass,   This little cow eats hay.

This little cow drinks water, This little cow runs away.

This little cow does nothing at all
But just sits down all day.

Well chase her,
Well chase her,
Well chase her
Away.

I'm a little teapot short and stout,
Here is my handle, here is my spout.
When I see the teacups hear me shout,
Tip me over and pour me out.

The eensy weensy spider
Went up the water spout.
Down came the rain
And washed the spider out.
Out came the sun
And dried up all the rain.
And the eensy weensy spider
Went up the spout again.

One little baby
Rocking in the tree,

Two little babies
Splashing in the sea,

Three little babies
Crawling on the floor,

Four little babies
Banging on the door,

Five little babies
Playing hide and seek,

Keep your eyes tight closed now,
Until I say . . . Peek!

Mary, Mary, quite contrary,
How does your garden grow?
With silver bells and cockle shells
And pretty maids all in a row.

Humpty Dumpty sat on a wall,
Humpty Dumpty had a great fall.
All the king's horses and all the king's men,
Couldn't put Humpty together again.

a great fall!

Jack and Jill went up the hill
To fetch a pail of water.
Jack fell down and broke his crown,
And Jill came tumbling after.

Up Jack got, and home did trot,
As fast as he could caper.
He went to bed to mend his head,
With vinegar and brown paper.

Dance to your daddy,
My little babby,
Dance to your daddy,
My little lamb.

You shall have a fishy
On a little dishy,
You shall have a fishy
When the boat comes in.

Diddle diddle dumpling, my son John
Went to bed with his trousers on.
One shoe off and the other shoe on,
Diddle diddle dumpling, my son John.

33

To market, to market,
To buy a fat pig.
Home again, home again,
Jiggety-jig.

To market, to market,
To buy a fat hog.
Home again, home again,
Jiggety-jog.

Mary had a little lamb,
Its fleece was white as snow,
And everywhere that Mary went,
The lamb was sure to go.

Ladybird, ladybird,
Fly away home.
Your house is on fire
And your children are gone.
All except one,
And that's little Ann,
And she crept under
The warming pan.

Polly, put the kettle on,
Polly, put the kettle on,
Polly, put the kettle on,
We'll all have tea.

Sukie, take it off again,
Sukie, take it off again,
Sukie, take it off again,
They've all gone away.

Pussy cat, pussy cat,
Where have you been?
I've been up to London
To look at the queen.

Pussy cat, pussy cat,
What did you there?
I frightened a little mouse
Under her chair.

help!

See-saw, Marjorie Daw,
Johnny shall have a new master.
He shall have but a penny a day,
Because he can't work any faster.

Hickory dickory dock,
The mouse ran up the clock.
The clock struck one,
The mouse ran down.
Hickory dickory dock.

Three blind mice, three blind mice,
See how they run, see how they run.
They all ran after the farmer's wife,
Who cut off their tails with a carving knife,
Did ever you see such a sight in your life
As three blind mice!

It's raining, it's pouring,
The old man is snoring.
He went to bed and bumped his head
And couldn't get up in the morning.

Baa baa, black sheep,
Have you any wool?
Yes sir, yes sir,
Three bags full.
One for the master,
One for the dame,
And one for the little boy
Who lives down the lane.

Hey diddle diddle, the cat and the fiddle,
The cow jumped over the moon.
The little dog laughed to see such fun
And the dish ran away with the spoon.

Little Bo-Peep has lost her sheep
And doesn't know where to find them.
Leave them alone and they'll come home,
Dragging their tails behind them.

Sing a song of sixpence,
A pocket full of rye,
Four and twenty blackbirds
Baked in a pie.
When the pie was opened
The birds began to sing.
Wasn't that a dainty dish
To set before the king!

The king was in his counting house,
Counting out his money,
The queen was in the parlor,
Eating bread and honey.
The maid was in the garden,
Hanging out the clothes,
When down came a blackbird
And pecked off her nose.

Little Miss Muffet sat on a tuffet,
Eating her curds and whey.
Along came a spider
Who sat down beside her
And frightened Miss Muffet away.

yeeuugh!

48

Little Jack Horner sat in a corner,
Eating his Christmas pie.
He put in his thumb and pulled out a plum
And said, "What a good boy am I!"

Old MacDonald had a farm,
E–i, e–i, o!
And on that farm he had some cows,
E–i, e–i, o!
With a *moo-moo* here,
And a *moo-moo* there,
Here a *moo*,
There a *moo*,
Everywhere a *moo-moo*.
Old MacDonald had a farm,
E–i, e–i, o!

Old MacDonald had a farm,
E–i, e–i, o!
And on that farm he had some pigs,
E–i, e–i, o!
With an *oink-oink* here,
And an *oink-oink* there,
Here an *oink*,
There an *oink*,
Everywhere an *oink-oink*.
Old MacDonald had a farm,
E–i, e–i, o!

Old MacDonald had a farm,
E–i, e–i, o!
And on that farm he had some . . .
hens (cluck-cluck)
ducks (quack-quack)
dogs (woof-woof), etc.

The cradle is warm
And there shall you sleep,
Safe and warm, little baby.
Angels shall come,
Stand closely to keep
Watch over you, little baby.
Bye-bye now, go to sleep,
So sweetly to sleep, little baby.

Hush-a-bye baby,
Thy cradle is green,
Father's a nobleman,
Mother's a queen.
Betty's a lady
And wears a gold ring,
John is a drummer
And drums for the king.
Boom-tiddy, boom-tiddy,
Boom, boom, boom.

boom bang

boom

Bye, Baby Bunting,
Daddy's gone a-hunting,
Gone to get a rabbit skin
To wrap his Baby Bunting in,
Bye, Baby Bunting.

Rock-a-bye baby on the tree top,
When the wind blows the cradle will rock.
When the bough breaks the cradle will fall,
And down will come cradle, baby and all.

treetops will be calm tonight

Lullaby, my pretty one,
Gone the day and set the sun.
Lullaby, my pretty one,
And sleep until the morning,
And sleep until the morning.

Sleep, baby, sleep,
Thy father tends the sheep,
Thy mother rocks the slumber-tree
And softly falls a dream for thee,
Sleep, baby, sleep.

Twinkle, twinkle, little star,
How I wonder what you are,
Up above the world so high,
Like a diamond in the sky.
Twinkle, twinkle, little star,
How I wonder what you are.

61

Golden slumbers kiss your eyes,
Smiles awake you when you rise.
Sleep, pretty darling, do not cry,
And I will sing a lullaby,
Lullaby, lullaby, lullaby.

Care you know not, therefore sleep,
While I o'er you watch do keep.
Sleep, pretty darling, do not cry,
And I will sing a lullaby,
Lullaby, lullaby, lullaby.

Sleep my baby,
Sleep my darling,
Baby, lullaby.
On your cradle
Moon is shining
Softly from the sky.

I shall sing
And tell you stories,
If you close your eyes.
Slumber sweetly
While I lull you,
Baby, lullaby.

MUSIC FOR LULLABIES

The cradle is warm

See page 53

The cra-dle is warm And there shall you sleep, Safe and warm, lit-tle ba-by.

An-gels shall come, stand close-ly to keep Watch o-ver you, lit-tle ba-by.

Bye-bye now, go to sleep, So sweet-ly to sleep, lit-tle ba-by.

Rock-a-bye baby

See page 58

Rock-a-bye ba-by on the tree top, When the wind

blows the cra-dle will rock. When the bough breaks the

cra-dle will fall, And down will come cra-dle, ba-by and all.

Hush-a-bye baby

See page 55

Hush-a-bye ba-by, Thy cra-dle is green, Fath-er's a no-ble-man, Moth-er's a queen.

Bet-ty's a lad-y And wears a gold ring, — John is a drum-mer and drums for the king.

Bye, Baby Bunting

See page 57

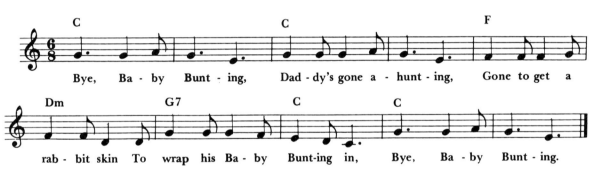

Bye, Ba-by Bunt-ing, Dad-dy's gone a-hunt-ing, Gone to get a

rab-bit skin To wrap his Ba-by Bunt-ing in, Bye, Ba-by Bunt-ing.

Lullaby, my pretty one

See page 59

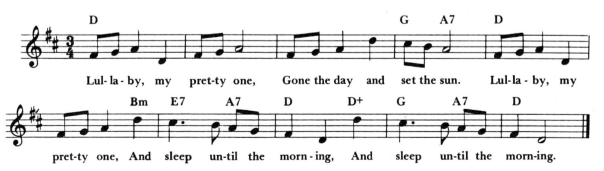

Lul-la-by, my pret-ty one, Gone the day and set the sun. Lul-la-by, my

pret-ty one, And sleep un-til the morn-ing, And sleep un-til the morn-ing.

Sleep, baby, sleep

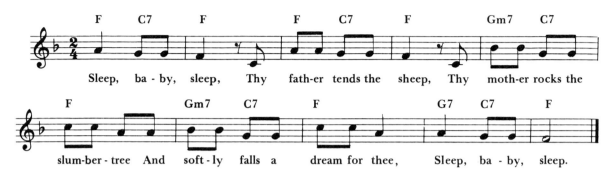

Sleep, ba - by, sleep, Thy fath-er tends the sheep, Thy moth-er rocks the
slum-ber - tree And soft - ly falls a dream for thee, Sleep, ba - by, sleep.

Twinkle, twinkle, little star

See page 61

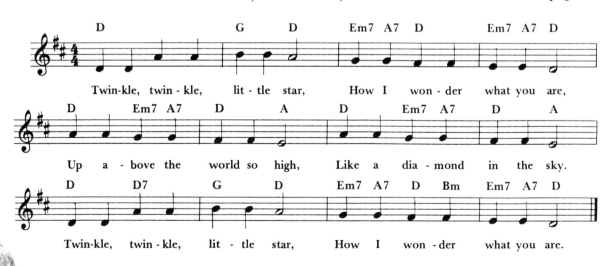

Twin-kle, twin - kle, lit - tle star, How I won - der what you are,
Up a - bove the world so high, Like a dia - mond in the sky.
Twin-kle, twin - kle, lit - tle star, How I won - der what you are.

68

Golden slumbers

See page 63

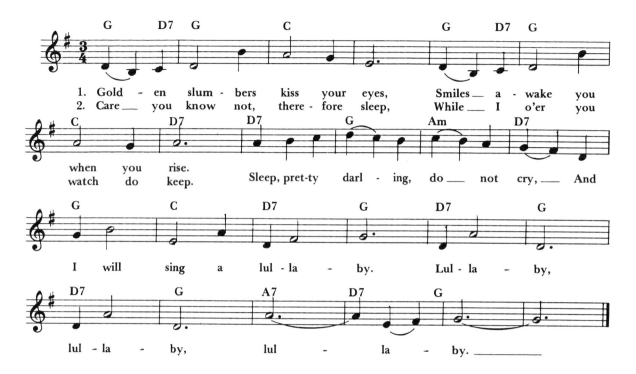

1. Gold - en slum - bers kiss your eyes, Smiles — a - wake you
2. Care — you know not, there - fore sleep, While — I o'er you

when you rise. Sleep, pret-ty darl - ing, do — not cry, — And
watch do keep.

I will sing a lul - la - by. Lul - la - by,

lul - la - by, lul - la - by. _____

Sleep my baby

See page 64

1. Sleep my ba - by, Sleep my darl - ing, Ba - by, lul - la - by.
2. I shall sing and tell you stor - ies, If you close your eyes.

On your cra - dle Moon is shin - ing Soft - ly from the sky.
Slum - ber sweet - ly while I lull you, Ba - by, lul - la - by.